D1385431

The Twelve Days of Christmas

Illustrated by John McIntosh
Written by June Williams

Dear Marina & Chris,

Here is a fun little book to give a
bit of Aussie to your christmas!

Have a lovely day

Thinking of you

Mandi Darren Stefanee Josie & Aidan

xxxxx
2008

HERRON BOOK DISTRIBUTORS

This edition first published 1992 by
HERRON BOOK DISTRIBUTORS
23 Archimedes Place, Murarrie
Qld. Australia 4172
Illustrations copyright © John McIntosh
Text copyright © June Williams
Music arranged by Andrew Bolt
Produced by Phoenix Offset, Hong Kong
Reprinted 2006, 2007, 2008

ISBN 0 947163 92 1

ON THE FIRST DAY OF CHRISTMAS
MY TRUE LOVE SENT TO ME.

AN EMU UP A GUM TREE.

An emu in trouble is sad to see,
Especially one who is caught in a tree.
It must have given her quite a fright
To hang from a limb — just out of sight.
For everyone knows that an emu can't fly,
Yet there she was, stranded up high.

ON THE SECOND DAY OF CHRISTMAS
MY TRUE LOVE SENT TO ME.

TWO PINK GALAHS.

There was no good reason, that I could see,
Why those two galahs should bother me.
I would have preferred to go on dreaming,
So I tried very hard to ignore their screaming.

ON THE THIRD DAY OF CHRISTMAS
MY TRUE LOVE SENT TO ME.

THREE JABIRUS.

A peck on the nose sure made me yelp,
But the kind jabirus were just trying to help.

ON THE FOURTH DAY OF CHRISTMAS
MY TRUE LOVE SENT TO ME.

FOUR KOOKABURRAS.

When it comes to helping others
You can't rely on kookaburras,
They don't do much but laugh all day —
Disturbing the peace then flying away.

ON THE FIFTH DAY OF CHRISTMAS
MY TRUE LOVE SENT TO ME.
FIVE KANGAROOS.

The kangaroos pointed. "Look there," they said
And tried in vain to turn my head.

ON THE SIXTH DAY OF CHRISTMAS
MY TRUE LOVE SENT TO ME.

SIX PLATYPUSES.

There was too much noise for me to stay.
So I jumped in the billabong to swim away.
Then found myself, without much fuss,
Brought back to shore by a platypus.

ON THE SEVENTH DAY OF CHRISTMAS
MY TRUE LOVE SENT TO ME.
SEVEN KOALAS CLIMBING.

Up and down,
And over, and under.
The climbing koalas began to wonder
Why it was I could not see
They needed a helping hand from me.

ON THE EIGHTH DAY OF CHRISTMAS
MY TRUE LOVE SENT TO ME.

EIGHT POSSUMS PLAYING.

The big-eyed possums ran this way and that,
And one did his best to remove my hat
Thinking, I'm sure, it would help me to see
The poor frightened emu up in the tree.

ON THE NINTH DAY OF CHRISTMAS.
MY TRUE LOVE SENT TO ME.

NINE WOMBATS WORKING.

The wombats grew tired of waiting for me,
They worried poor emu might fall from the tree.
"We'll make a ladder from the broken crate,
And bring her down before it's too late."

ON THE TENTH DAY OF CHRISTMAS
MY TRUE LOVE SENT TO ME.

TEN LIZARDS LEAPING.

Pushing, pulling,
And leaping high,
At last I knew the reason why
Those lizards would not let me be
For I SAW the emu caught in the tree.

ON THE ELEVENTH DAY OF CHRISTMAS
MY TRUE LOVE SENT TO ME.

ELEVEN NUMBATS NAGGING.

I climbed the ladder carefully
And reached up high into the tree,
While, from below, there came a call,
"We've a parachute here in case you fall."

ON THE TWELFTH DAY OF CHRISTMAS
MY TRUE LOVE SENT TO ME.
TWELVE PARROTS PRATTLING.

The parrots watched, all perched in line,
And one squawked out, "You're doing fine."
It's not every day a bloke like me
Rescues an emu stuck up a tree.

Now Mabel's present is wrapped up tight.
It took some time to get it right.
I'm sending a card and a photo too
Of my new found friends and that silly emu.

Merry Christmas
— love Dave

THE TWELVE DAYS OF CHRISTMAS

Arranged by Andrew Bolt.

ON THE FIRST DAY OF CHRISTMAS MY TRUE LOVE SENT TO ME

An emu up a gum tree
Two pink galahs
Three jabirus
Four kookaburras
Five kangaroos
Six platypuses
Seven koalas climbing
Eight possums playing
Nine wombats working
Ten lizards leaping
Eleven numbats nagging
Twelve parrots prattling